To My Falling Leaves
the story of Autumn

written & illustrated by

Janae Dueck

to those in need of
encouragement.

In the fall, we all know trees begin to lose their leaves.
1, 2, 3, they break. Yellow, orange, and a little of gold; a wonderful
season except for one whose heart grows cold.

Here is Autumn, a sapling of a tree
saddened at the sight,
of losing his beautiful leaves
for the coming winter night.

He recalls the other seasons,
summer, winter, spring,
when he felt so very happy,
so alive in what they bring.

"Oh how the winter time
was one of many cheers,
presents, songs, and traditions
from so many years.

My branches decorated
shimmery reds and sparkling whites,
admired for my beauty,
glowing with all those lights!"

Autumn watches more leaves float away, and only wishes for them to stay.

"To my falling leaves," he says, "I hope and I pray...
for you to be used, for someone in someway."

"Remember my time in the spring," he sighs,
"the rain, the sun, and bright blue skies?

Where lovers held close
sharing hearts and sunset kisses,
such blissful days,
why this Autumn surely misses."

As each moment passes, the tree grows bear. How could losing leaves be fair?

"To my falling leaves," he says, "I do hope and pray...
for you to be used, for someone in someway."

Autumn thinks of summer, a season never to forget.
"I was home to many birds," he laughs,
"singing songs of sweet duet!"

I had kids swinging
and climbing all around me so.
Where are they now? Oh where did they go?"

More leaves break. If only the wind would withhold, Autumn's remaining leaves before his heart becomes too cold.

"To my falling leaves," he longs, "I truly wish and pray...
for you to be used, for someone in someway."

Then, from over the hilltop, comes a girl and her dad;
a spark of excitement, making the tree a bit
more glad.

Autumn wonders, so curious as
can be, "they carry a big, long stick...
should they ever come to me?"

Indeed the two came, smiles and all,
raking Autumn's leaves into a pile so very tall.

Once stacked to the most perfect height, the girl disappears, only to run back with all her might!

And one giant leap, the sky now painted of yellow, orange, and a
little of gold, of leaves flying everywhere, why this kind of fun was
never told!

The tree laughs, a chuckle that showers the two with more and more,
leave upon leaves, of what this fall season was always meant for.

For trees like Autumn,
to discover how much good
one can give,

in bringing joy to a season,
that others could share and live!

"To my falling leaves," Autumn smiles, "I know and I now say...
gone away but not forgotten, you were used in a special way."

the end.

Thank you for picking up my book! I'm Janae and I am delighted to see this story finally come to life. When I was just 14 years old, I sketched out the idea of "Autumn the tree", dreaming of the day it would become a published children's book. Well, at 20 years of age, here it is!

I hope you enjoy this story as it has brought a lot of truth to my life. Through the eyes of a tree in a season like fall, we can all tend to feel as though we are losing our "leaves" at various times in our lives. Seasons of prosperity will come and go, but when a season of loss, pain, or dismay comes around, it may not necessarily feel the greatest. In fact, we can probably relate to Autumn's beginnings of feeling forgotten and alone. But when his fallen leaves bring laughter to a little girl and her dad, Autumn's idea of fall becomes something truly special. He discovers it is in the falling leaves where others can be encouraged and in return, this lifts his heart! Likely so, our life's aches can also be but a catalyst to inspire others. This book was written in time of hurt, but it stands as an example of the joy found despite the lost "leaves". The smiles it brings, the message it delivers; makes it all the more worth it. And through this story of Autumn, my hope is that you can make your own discovery of impact. So when found in a season like fall, you too can say to *your* falling "leaves"--you will be of great encouragement to someone in someway!

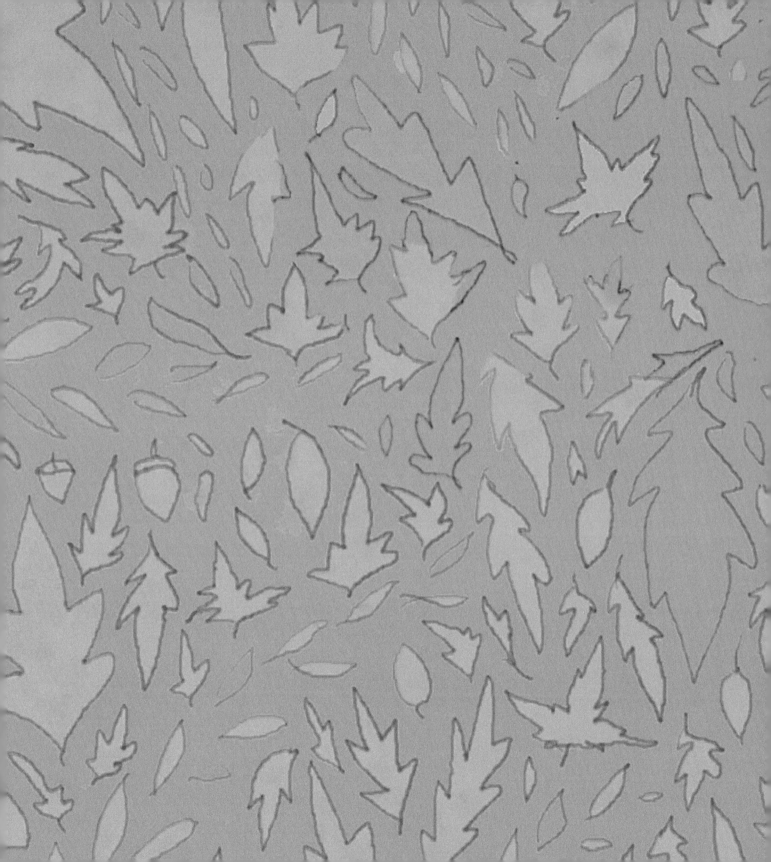

Made in the USA
San Bernardino, CA
30 December 2015